Souvenir Press

Jane is Adopted

by Althea

illustrated by Isabel Pearce

Published by Souvenir Press Ltd 43 Great Russell Street London WC1B 3PA

© 1980 Dinosaur Publications Ltd   ISBN 285 62457 1

Reprinted 1984

Printed in Spain by Grijelmo, S.A. Bilbao

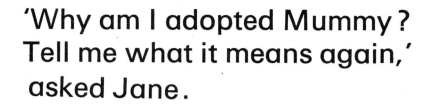

'Why am I adopted Mummy?
Tell me what it means again,'
asked Jane.

'Come and sit on my lap,'
said Mummy,
'And I will explain.'

'Daddy and I wanted
very much to have a child
to live with us
and be part of our family.
But a baby did not grow
inside me,
so we decided to try
and adopt a child.'

'We went to see a lady
called Miss Jones
to ask about adopting
a child.'

'*Adopt* means to look after
and be a Mummy and Daddy
to someone else's child
for always.'

'Miss Jones came to see us
and asked us lots of questions.
She looked round the house
to see how comfortable it was.'

'Miss Jones wanted to be sure
that we would be good parents
and that we would love
and look after a child
who came to live with us.'

ROSE PINK

'We made a bedroom
ready for a child.
But lots of people
want to adopt children
so we had to wait
a very long time.'

'At last Miss Jones
came to see us again,
to tell us she thought she had
found the right child for us.'

'We went to see you in your
foster home. You have
such a lovely smile, Jane,
we loved you straight away.'

'Your parents were not married
and they didn't have a home
where you could all live together.
They were very happy when
they knew that you were
going to live with us.'

'We told them that
we would love you always
and look after you.'

'It's nice that you have dark hair
and brown eyes
just like your mother.'

'We were very happy and excited
when you came to live with us,
now we could all
be a family together.
We are your Mummy and
Daddy now.'

'So you see *adopted* means
to belong to a family.
We all belong together
and we love you very much.'

' I am glad that
Mummy and Daddy
adopted me.' thought
Jane.